The
KINGFISHER
Treasury of

Stories
for
Beginning
Readers

KINGFISHER
Larousse Kingfisher Chambers Inc.
80 Maiden Lane, New York, New York 10038
www.kingfisherpub.com

First published in 2001
2 4 6 8 10 9 7 5 3 1
1TR/0801/TIMS/IGS(MAR)/130MA

LIBRARY OF CONGRESS CATALOGING–IN–PUBLICATION DATA
has been applied for.

ISBN 0-7534-5410-6

Printed in China

The
KINGFISHER
Treasury of
Stories
for
Beginning
Readers

Introduction by Wendy Cooling

KINGFISHER

NEW YORK

Contents

Introduction

You've just picked up a book of really good stories. They are great to read in many ways—on your own, to a grown-up, or with a friend. Now that you are beginning to read by yourself, you can choose how you want to read stories:

★ You can read silently to yourself.
★ Sometimes it is helpful to read out loud to yourself. Hearing the sounds of words can help bring the story to life. Words like **thump** and **crash** are fun to read very loudly.
★ You may like an audience; reading stories to others can be very enjoyable.
★ Sharing the reading is good too. Reading the part of a character or taking turns reading a page means that you get to be both listener and reader.

To begin with, look at the contents page and choose the story you would like to read first. Turn to the title page for that story. Can you tell from the title and the pictures what kind of story it will be?

★ Read the story to yourself. Take it slowly. Look at the pictures for help when you come to a difficult word. Look carefully at the beginning of the word and then at the whole word.
★ Remember, it doesn't matter if you don't understand every word. It matters that you can read enough of the words and the pictures to enjoy the story.
★ Pause when you come to a comma or a period. Stopping or slowing down in the right places helps make sense of the words.

* Next read the story to family or friends. They will be pleased to hear you enjoying reading.
* Try to read with expression—make those **crash** words really **CRASH!** You will feel great when your listeners laugh at a joke.
* If you get stuck, ask for help and then go on with the story. It's always better to ask about a few words than to miss the point of the story.

As you read more you will manage harder words and need less help. You will be surprised to find that you learn a lot of interesting new words. And in all the stories you can learn something about feelings and about the importance of friends.

Enjoy reading!

Wendy Cooling

Wendy Cooling

The Giant Postman

SALLY GRINDLEY
WENDY SMITH

Chapter One

"He's coming!" screamed a little girl.

"He's coming!" shouted the
ice cream man.

"He's coming!" shouted
the window cleaner.

Children dropped their
schoolbags and ran.

Shoppers dropped their
shopping and ran.

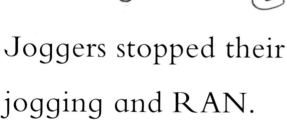

Joggers stopped their
jogging and RAN.

Soon, the street was empty.

It was so quiet you could hear a pin drop.

Then there was a loud thump.

And another. And another.

THUMP! THUMP! THUMP!

Great big boots cracked the

sidewalk.

Great big boots shook the houses.

Behind closed curtains, people
shivered with fear.

"Please don't have any mail for us,"
they whispered.

THUMP! THUMP! THUMP!

The Giant Postman was coming.

Chapter Two

Billy and his mom lived at Number 24.

"Get under the table!" screamed Billy's mom.

But Billy stood at the window and watched the Giant Postman stomping from door to door.

THUMP! THUMP! THUMP!

The Giant Postman was right outside Billy's house.

BANG! BANG! BANG!

He pounded on the door.

"I have a package for you,"

he bellowed.

"Just leave it outside, please," called Billy's mom. "Oh, no," replied the Giant Postman. "I don't want it to be stolen."

BANG! BANG! BANG!

Billy quickly opened the door and hid behind it.

"Here you are!" bellowed the Giant Postman, and he dropped the package on the floor.

Then he stomped off down the street.

THUMP! THUMP! THUMP!

"Has he gone?" whispered Billy's mom.

Billy peered around the door.

"Yes, he's gone," he said.

Then Billy walked out into the street.

The street was still empty.

Mr. White's front gate was hanging off its hinges.

Mr. Homer's cabbages were trampled to the ground.

Mrs. Atwell's cat was on the roof of her house, quivering with fright.

One by one the villagers appeared. "Is it safe?" they asked.

"Yes," said Billy, "he's gone.

But it's time we did something.

Getting letters is supposed to be fun."

"We're all too scared to do anything,"

they said.

"Well, I'm not," said Billy.

"I'm going to write a letter to the postman and ask him to stop frightening us."

The crowd gasped.

"And I'm going to deliver it myself!"

Chapter Three

That same day, Billy sat down and wrote his letter.

Dear Mr. Postman,
My name is Billy and I live in the village.
I am writing to ask you to please stop frightening us.

Mr. Homer is very upset about his cabbages and Mrs. Atwell's cat won't come down from the roof. We would like to be friends with you.
Best wishes,
Billy

He wrote "Mr. Postman" on an envelope and put the letter inside. Then Billy set off to the woods where the Giant Postman lived. "Don't go, Billy!" cried his mom.

BY HAND
Mr. Postman
The Woods

"Don't go, Billy!" cried the villagers.

But Billy kept going,

past the bakery . . .

past the shoe store . . .

past the school . . .

on and on, until at last he reached
the woods.

The woods were very dark.

Billy heard strange noises.

CRICK! CRACK! RUSTLE!

He began to feel frightened.

CRICK!

He wanted to go back.

CRACK!

But he made himself go on.

RUSTLE!

Faster and faster he went, until . . .

at last he came to a clearing.

There stood the Giant Postman's
great big house.

Billy was surprised to see that
the yard was full of flowers.

He walked up to the door.

Chapter Four

TAP! TAP! TAP!

Billy knocked on the Giant

Postman's door.

Nobody came.

TAP! TAP! TAP!

He knocked a little louder.

At last, he heard footsteps—

SHUFFLE, SHUFFLE, SHUFFLE.

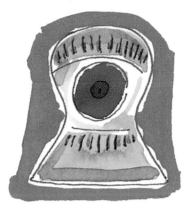 Then Billy saw a giant
eye peeping through
the keyhole.

"What do you want?"
bellowed the Giant Postman.

"I b-b-brought a letter,"
Billy stammered.

"What do you mean?" said the
Giant Postman.
"*I* deliver the letters."

"It's a letter for
you," said Billy.

Slowly, slowly
the door opened.
The Giant Postman stared
at Billy.

He took the envelope and peered at it.

Slowly, slowly he pulled out the letter.

He read it over and over again.

Billy shifted his feet nervously
on the doorstep.

He was all alone with
the Giant Postman.

Billy felt very scared.

Then he noticed that
the Giant Postman
was wearing slippers
and had holes in the
elbows of his sweater.

Billy looked at his
face and thought
he saw him smile.

But the Giant Postman turned away
and closed the door without a word.

Billy ran all the way home,
through the dark woods . . .
on and on, until at last he reached
his house.

"Oh, Billy!" cried his mom.
"Thank goodness you're safe."
"He read my letter," said Billy,
"but he didn't say a word.
I hope I haven't made him angry."

But that night Billy remembered
the yard full of flowers.
He remembered the slippers,
and the woolly sweater with holes.
The Giant Postman didn't seem
so frightening without his uniform
and his great big boots.

Chapter Five

The next morning, Billy looked
out of his window.

It wasn't long before he saw
people running to hide.

THUMP! THUMP! THUMP!

The Giant Postman was coming.

Great big boots cracked the
sidewalk.

Great big boots shook the houses.

THUMP! THUMP! THUMP!

The Giant Postman was right outside

Billy's house.

"Get under the table!" screamed

Billy's mom.

But Billy opened the window.

"Good morning, Mr. Postman," he said.

From his bag the Giant Postman pulled an

enormous envelope.

"I have a letter for you," he said.

Then he stomped off down the

empty street.

THUMP! THUMP! THUMP!

Billy ran downstairs.

His hands shook as he took the

letter out of the envelope.

BILLY

He read:

Dear Billy,
Thank you for your letter.
I've never gotten one
before. I don't mean to
frighten people. I'm sorry
about Mr. Homer's
cabbages. I'm afraid
I'm clumsy in my boots.
Will you write to me
again tomorrow, please?
It's my birthday.
Your friend,
Mr. Postman

Billy smiled and ran out into
the street.

"It's all right," he said, waving
the letter. "You can come out."
He danced up and down
until a crowd gathered
around him.

Then he showed them the letter.

"Never got a letter!"
said Mr. Homer.

"Poor thing,"
said Mrs. Atwell.

"He sounds a
little lonely,"
said Mr. White.

"I don't think he's scary
at all," said a little girl.
"I'm going to make him
a birthday card."

"I guess he can't help being clumsy in his big boots," said Billy.

Then he had an idea.

Chapter Six

That night the villagers didn't sleep.
Lights burned in all the houses.
Delicious smells came from the
bakery, and loud noises came
from the shoe store—
BANG! THUMP! RRRRR!

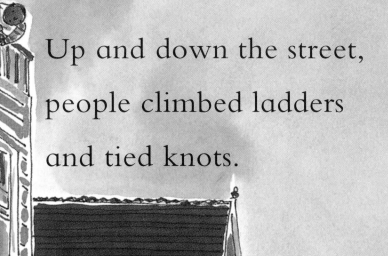

Up and down the street,
people climbed ladders
and tied knots.

Just as dawn broke,

everything was ready.

The villagers stood by their windows

and waited. And waited.

THUMP! THUMP! THUMP!

The Giant Postman was coming.

THUMP!

THUMP!

The great big boots

stopped in their tracks.

The Giant Postman

stared.

And stared.

Banners and balloons hung from every house and from every lamppost. The banners read:

TO OUR POSTMAN, A VERY HAPPY BIRTHDAY!

The village band began to play.

DRUM! DRUM! DRUM!

TOOT! TOOT! TOOT-TOOT!

The villagers rushed into the

street, waving birthday cards.

Billy came out of the shoe store
pulling a cart. On top of the
cart was the biggest package
you have ever seen.

"HAPPY BIRTHDAY,
MR. POSTMAN," said Billy.

"This present is from all of us."

Gently, the Giant Postman pulled off the paper and lifted the lid of the great big box.

"Just what I've always wanted!" he gasped.

The Giant Postman held up a

great big pair of new sneakers.

"Try them on!" the villagers cried.

So, he tried them on.

"They're perfect," he said.

"They're so soft and springy."

He walked up and down

without a single THUMP.

Then the Giant Postman
smiled a great big smile.
The villagers cheered.

"Time for a party," Billy yelled.

"Time for a party," everyone cried.

The Giant Postman danced down the street.

"Time for a party!" he bellowed with delight.

"This is the very best birthday ever!"

Crocodile and Alligator Bake a Cake

NICOLA MOON
ANDY ELLIS

Crocodile and Alligator
Bake a Cake

Crocodile and Alligator were baking a cake.
Crocodile had his grandma's recipe book
and an enormous mixing bowl.

Alligator was opening all the cupboards.

"We need some flour," said Crocodile.

"What's flour?" said Alligator.

"It's white and soft and dusty,"
said Crocodile.

"And it's in a blue bag."
As he spoke, a blue bag
wobbled
and toppled
and landed POOF!
on the floor
at Alligator's feet.

"Like this?" asked Alligator.

"Yes," said Crocodile. "That's flour."

Crocodile put four big spoonfuls

of flour into the bowl.

Alligator swept up the mess.

"We need some eggs," said Crocodile.

"How many?" asked Alligator.

"Two," said Crocodile. "Two large eggs."

Alligator picked out two big, brown eggs

from the carton.

"I saw someone juggle eggs once,"

he said. "Like this . . ."

SPLAT! SPLOSH!

Alligator wasn't very good at juggling.

Luckily, there were two more eggs left.
Crocodile cracked the eggs
against the side of the bowl,
opened the shells,
and let the eggs
drop onto
the flour.

"You should be more careful, Alligator."
"I will," said Alligator,
cleaning up the mess.

"We need some margarine," said Crocodile.

"Where will I find that?" asked Alligator.

"In the fridge," said Crocodile.

"In a large, white tub."

Alligator opened the fridge

and took out the large, white tub.

He tried to open the lid.

It was very tight.

"Will you open it for me, please?"

Crocodile pulled
and tugged
and heaved
and . . . PLOP!

The lid shot off
and Crocodile
dropped the tub
on the floor.
Upside down.

61

"You should be more careful, Crocodile,"
laughed Alligator.

"Very funny," said Crocodile,
and he picked up the tub.

Luckily, there was still some margarine left.

Alligator wiped up the mess.

"We need some sugar," said Crocodile.

"I know where the sugar is," said Alligator

"I like sugar."

He reached up and carefully lifted down

the container marked SUGAR.

"Be careful—don't slip . . ."

said Crocodile.

CRASH!

It was too late.

Alligator sat on the floor

looking miserable,

covered in sticky sugar.

"I don't think I'm very good

at making cakes," he said.

"You just need to be more careful,"

said Crocodile.

He measured

what was left of the sugar.

Alligator looked sadly at the mess.

"All we need now are some raisins,"
said Crocodile.

"You can measure them if you like,"
he added.

Alligator cheered up.

He measured the raisins
and put them into a little dish.

"We add them later," explained Crocodile.

"May I taste one?" asked Alligator.

"Just one," said Crocodile,

who was busy plugging in the mixer.

Alligator ate a raisin.

Then another one.

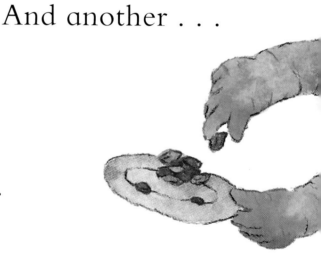

And another . . .

Then just one more.

"We're ready to mix it,"
said Crocodile.
"Stand back!"

Crocodile switched on the mixer.

WHOOSH!

The flour and eggs

and margarine and sugar

spun around in the bowl so fast

it made Alligator dizzy.

"Is that really going to turn into a cake?"

asked Alligator,

looking at the creamy mixture.

"A delicious cake," said Crocodile.

He switched off the mixer.

"Now it's time for you

to stir in the raisins."

Crocodile poured
the mixture into
a big, round cake pan

and put it into the oven to bake.

"Now we can clean up the mess," he said.

"And when we're done
the cake will be ready."

They mopped

and swept

and wiped

and polished the floor.

Crocodile washed

the mixing bowl and the spoon

and cleaned the mixer.

"Mmmm!" said Alligator.

"I smell something good."

"I think the cake is ready,"

said Crocodile.

He lifted it out of the oven very carefully.

When the cake was cool,

Crocodile cut two huge slices,

and poured two glasses of lemonade.

"Scrumptious!" said Alligator.

"I'm good at *eating* cakes!"

"There don't seem to be many raisins in it,"
said Crocodile.

"May I have another piece?"
asked Alligator.

"Only if you sweep up the crumbs,"
said Crocodile.

"Just look at the mess you're making!"

Joe Lion's Big Boots

KARA MAY

JONATHAN ALLEN

Chapter One

Joe Lion was small.

He was the smallest in his class.

He couldn't even reach the

goldfish to feed it.

"It's only me who

can't reach,"

said Joe.

He was the smallest in his family, too.

Big Brother Ben could reach

the cookie jar, easy peasy.

Sister Susan could reach it

easy peasy, too.

But Joe? He couldn't reach it,

not even on tiptoe.

"I'm fed up with being small,"
he said to Mom and Dad.
"I was small once," said Dad.
"You'll grow bigger one day,"
Mom told him.

But Joe wanted to be bigger NOW.

"I'll WISH myself bigger," he said.

He shut his eyes and wished.

He was still wishing when

he went to bed.

But the next morning, he was

the same small Joe Lion.

"Wishing hasn't made me bigger," he said.

"I'll have to think of something else."

He went to the big comfy chair

where he did his thinking.

What was this on the chair?

 It was Mom's new book,

How to Grow Sunflowers.

"Aha!" grinned Joe.

"That gives me an idea."

Big Brother Ben had a *How to . . .*

book—just the book Joe wanted.

He raced up to Ben's room.

On the bed he saw the book:

How to Build Yourself a Bigger Body.

Joe read through it in a flash.

To get bigger, he had to eat

a lot of food like pasta.

Mmm! Yum!

"I have to work out, too," said Joe.

"I know where I can do that!"

Chapter Two

Joe ran all the way to Gus Gorilla's gym.

Gus was big. Very big!

"Working out seems to do the trick," thought Joe.

"I can't wait to start," he said to Gus.

"What do I have to do?"

"You stand on this and run!" said Gus.

Joe ran on the treadmill.

Then it was onto the exercise bike.

After that, it was the rowing machine.

Puff! Puff! Puff!
Pant! Pant! Pant!

"Now, lift these weights, young Joe," said Gus. "Lift them good and high."

Joe's arms ached. His legs ached.

Even his little finger ached!

But he wanted to be bigger.

He picked up the weights.

He lifted them good and high . . .

until a weight fell . . .

CRASH!

"Yikes! It nearly hit my foot. That's the
end of working out for me," said Joe.
But he was still determined to get bigger.

"Now I'm not working out," said Joe, "I'll do lots of extra eating to make up for it." Wherever Joe went, whatever Joe was doing, it was: MUNCH! CRUNCH! GOBBLE! At home:

MUNCH! CRUNCH! GOBBLE!

At school:

MUNCH! CRUNCH! GOBBLE!

On the bus:

MUNCH! CRUNCH! GOBBLE!

Even in the tub:

MUNCH! CRUNCH! GOBBLE!

"I have to be bigger by now," said Joe at last. He went to take a look in the mirror. He didn't like what he saw. "Oh, no," he groaned. After all that working out and eating, he was bigger, yes. Bigger-WIDER!

"But I want to be bigger-TALLER!"
said Joe.

Sister Susan had gotten bigger-taller
in just five minutes.

He asked her how she did it.

"I put on my high-heeled shoes,"
she said.

"Aha!" said Joe.

"That gives me an idea . . . !"

Chapter Three

Joe rushed into Ernie Elephant's shoe shop.

"I need some shoes to make me bigger-taller," he said.

"Boots are best for that," said Ernie.

Joe tried on a lot of boots, but none of them made him as bigger-taller as he wanted.

"I can make you some," said Ernie.
"But it'll cost you, AND you have
to pay in advance."

Joe paid Ernie. "It's all the money
I have, but it will be worth it,"
said Joe.

"I'll bring them over—delivery
is free," said Ernie.

Joe couldn't wait for the new boots to arrive.

But at last, here was Ernie. Now for the BIG MOMENT.

Joe took the lid off the box.

He took out his new boots and put them on.

"This is more like it!" said Joe.

He went to show the others.

"Surprise, surprise!

I'm a lot bigger-taller now."

They were surprised all right—

too surprised to speak!

Bigger-taller Joe could do a lot of things he couldn't do before.

He could reach the hall light. He turned it on and off—just because he could!

He could reach to swing from the rope.

He could see over Gus Gorilla's fence.

His new boots made a great noise, too!

CLOMP! CLOMP! CLOMP!

Chapter Four

Joe made his way to the bus stop.

"I like this bigger-taller me!"
he said.

He was closer to the
sky and could feel
the sun better.

He saw the bus coming,

and ran to catch it—or tried to!

In his Clomping Clompers, he could

only: CLOMP! CLOMP! CLOMP!

The bus went without him.

Joe was late for school.

Mrs. Croc wasn't pleased.

"I'm sorry, Mrs. Croc," said Joe.

"It was my Clomping Clompers."

"May I feed the goldfish?" he asked.

But the goldfish was already fed.

At recess, his friends were playing soccer. Joe was good at scoring goals.

But not in his Clomping Clompers.

Joe was glad to get home.

"Cookie jar, here I come!"

He reached it, easy peasy.

Now it was time to watch his favorite

TV show, *Super Lion in Space*.

But then Mom said, "Hang up your

coat, Joe. You can reach the hook

in your Clomping Clompers."

And that was just the start of it.

Joe could reach a lot of things
he couldn't reach when he was
small Joe Lion.
Like the kitchen sink:
"It's your turn to do the dishes,"
said Big Brother Ben.

Like the toy shelf:

"You can put your toys up there yourself," said Sister Susan.

Doing the dishes! Cleaning up!

"It's all I seem to do these days!" said Joe.

But he couldn't do much else in his Clomping Clompers.

Later, Joe's friends were off to the park.

"Are you coming, Joe?" they asked.

Joe shook his head.

He couldn't join in the games.

"I can only clomp!" he said.

"I'm going for a walk."

109

Joe clomped off down the street.

CLOMP! CLOMP! CLOMP!

But what was up with Jeff Giraffe?

"He looks like he's in trouble!"

said Joe.

Chapter Five

Joe soon discovered that Jeff

WAS in trouble.

"Goofy giraffe that I am,

I've locked myself out," he said.

"I came outside to pick some flowers,

and I left the bathwater running!"

Joe saw the problem at once.

Left to itself, the tub would overflow

and Jeff's house would be flooded!

Joe spotted the bathroom window—
it was open!

"You can get in up there," he said.

Jeff pushed his head through the window.

"But my bottom half won't fit,"
said Jeff. "The window's too small."

"Leave it to me," said Joe.

He knew what he must do.
First, off with his Clomping
Clompers.

Now, it was
Super Joe Lion
to the rescue!
Up the downspout.
In through the
window.

The water was rising fast—

and a lot of soapy bubbles with it!

"I have to do something!" Joe reached

for the stopper.

It was too far down.

He would have to go in!

He got up on the side of the tub
and jumped.

SPLASH!

He couldn't see through the bubbles
and he was running out of breath.
But he had to get to the stopper.
"Got it!" He pulled the stopper and
out it came.
The water gurgled down.
GLUG! GLUG! GLUG!
Joe whooshed the bubbles
out the window.

Then he slid back down
the downspout.
He saw a crowd had gathered.
Mom and Dad were there, and
Brother Ben and Sister Susan
and Gus and Ernie and
Mrs. Croc and all his friends.
They were waiting for news.

Quickly, Joe told them:

"Jeff's house is safe from flooding with bathwater and it's safe from bubbles, too!"

They all gave a cheer.

"Hurrah for Super Joe Lion!"

Joe felt very proud.

He was Super Joe Lion—just
as he was. He didn't need his
Clomping Clompers.

"My clomping days are over," said Joe. "Being me is best. I don't want to be bigger . . . well, not yet!"

JJ Rabbit
and the
Adventure

NICOLA MOON
ANT PARKER

JJ Rabbit and the Adventure

"I'm bored!" said JJ one day.

"I feel like going on an adventure."

"An adventure?" asked Mole.

"What's that?"

"It's when you go somewhere new,

and something exciting happens,"

said JJ. "Owl told me."

"I think I feel like going on
an adventure too," said Mole.

"Let's go together!" said JJ,
and scampered off into the woods.
"Wait for me!" called Mole.

They bumped into Squirrel.
"Where are you two going
in such a hurry?" he asked.
"We're looking for an adventure,"
said Mole.
"Looking for a what?"
asked Squirrel.

"An adventure," said JJ.

"It's when you go somewhere new and something exciting happens."

"Can I come too?" said Squirrel.

"Only if you don't run too fast," said Mole.

The animals followed a path
that twisted and turned
through the woods.

"Are we there yet?" panted Mole.

"Not yet," said JJ.

"How will we know when we are?"
said Mole.

"When we are somewhere new,"
said Squirrel.

"When something exciting happens,"
said JJ.

The animals walked until they
reached the end of the woods.

But they didn't find an adventure.

Then they walked past a field of wheat,

and through a field of turnips.

But nothing exciting happened.

They walked for miles and miles.

They walked past a field of cows,

and over a little bridge.

"I'm tired of looking for an adventure,"
said Squirrel.

"I didn't think adventures were so far away," said Mole.

"Can we stop for a rest now, JJ?" asked Squirrel. "JJ . . .?"

Squirrel looked back along the path.

JJ had disappeared!

Mole and Squirrel

looked behind trees . . .

and under bushes . . .

but there was no JJ.

Suddenly, Squirrel stood still.

"Listen!" he said. "What's that?"

"What's what?" said Mole.

"Ssshh!" whispered Squirrel.

A small voice was calling,

"Help! Help me!"

Mole and Squirrel followed the voice

back along the path to the bridge.

"Help!" it called again.

The voice was getting louder.

"It's JJ!" cried Squirrel.

Mole and Squirrel looked

down over the bridge.

There was poor JJ,

stuck fast in the mud.

"Help!" he squealed.

"I can't move!"

"It's all right," cried Mole.

"We'll save you!"

Squirrel found a long, strong stick and held it out to JJ.

JJ grabbed the stick with his paws and held on tight.

Mole and Squirrel held the other end and pulled.

And pulled . . .

and pulled . . . .

At last there was a loud

SQUELCH!

and an even louder

PLOP!

and JJ was free.

"Poor JJ!" said Mole. "What happened?"

"I just came to get a drink." JJ shivered.

"I didn't know the mud would be so

SQUELCHY."

The sun was sinking

lower and lower in the sky.

It was starting to get dark.

"I don't want to look for

adventures anymore," said JJ.

"I just want to go home."

"I don't think there *are* any

adventures out here," said Mole.

"Which way is home?" asked JJ.

"Over the bridge, past a field of wheat,

and through a field of cows,"

said Squirrel.

"Or was it over the bridge,

past a field of cows,

and then through a field of turnips?"

said Mole, slowly.

"You mean you don't know?" said JJ.

"You mean we're *lost*?"

Mole shivered.

"I don't like being lost," she said.

"Especially not in the dark,"

said Squirrel.

"I want to go home!" wailed JJ.

It was getting darker and darker.

Suddenly they heard

a strange rustling noise.

"What's that?" whispered Squirrel.

"It's a wolf!" cried Mole.

There was more rustling,

followed by a swooshing noise.

"Help!" squealed JJ.

There was another swoosh,
and Owl swooped down from the sky.
"Oh, Owl!" said JJ. "We thought you
were a wolf! We're lost."
"Squirrel doesn't know the way
home," said Mole.
"Nor does Mole!" said Squirrel.
"Oh dear, oh dear," chuckled Owl.
"It's lucky I flew by!"

Three very tired and bedraggled
animals followed Owl as
he led the way.

Soon they were nearly home.

"Look, there's Badger!" said Mole.

Badger was snuffling about,

looking for slugs.

"Where have you all been?" he said.

"We were looking for an adventure,"

said JJ.

"But we couldn't find one," said Mole.

"We walked for miles," said JJ,

"then I got stuck in the mud!"

"Then we got lost," said Squirrel,

"and Mole thought there was a wolf."

"But Owl came and saved us!"

cried Mole, happily.

"So you see," said Squirrel,

"there wasn't time for an adventure."

"No," said JJ, with a big yawn,

"but if we get up early tomorrow,

then we might find a *real* adventure."

Mr. Cool

JACQUELINE WILSON
STEPHEN LEWIS

Chapter One

Ricky wanted to be a rock star.

He was excellent at singing.

He was excellent at dancing.

He looked excellent, too.

Ricky had floppy, fair hair
that fell into his blue eyes.

Ricky always wore blue denim.

Ricky looked cool.

Micky wanted to be a rock star.

He was terrific at singing.

He was terrific at dancing.

He looked terrific, too.

Micky had long, red hair
and wicked green eyes.

Micky always wore black.

Micky looked cool.

Nicky wanted to be a rock star.

He was fantastic at singing.

He was fantastic at dancing.

He looked fantastic, too.

Nicky had curly, black hair
and big brown eyes.

Nicky always wore leather.

Nicky looked cool.

Kevin wanted to be a rock star.

He wasn't great at singing.

He wasn't great at dancing.

He didn't look great either.

Kevin had straight, mousy hair
and gray eyes.

Kevin always wore a sweater,
knitted by his grandma, and track pants.

Kevin didn't look cool.

But he had a great smile.

Ricky and Micky and Nicky formed a band.

"Can I be in the band, too?" asked Kevin.

Ricky and Micky and Nicky weren't sure.

"You're a nice guy, Kevin. But you're not that great at singing," said Ricky.

Kevin smiled bravely.

Ricky felt bad.

"We do like you, Kevin. But you're not that great at dancing," said Micky.

Kevin smiled bravely.

Micky felt bad.

"You can't help it, Kevin.
You just don't look cool,"
said Nicky.
Kevin smiled bravely.
Nicky felt bad.

"I wish I could be in your band,"

said Kevin, still smiling.

"Come on, you guys.

Let me be in the band.

I'll try hard at singing.

I'll try hard at dancing..

I'll try hard to look cool."

Ricky and Micky and Nicky

still weren't sure.

"My grandma has a basement," said Kevin.

"We could practice there.

My grandma won't mind."

Ricky and Micky and Nicky

didn't have a good place to practice.

153

Ricky lived in a small house.
Ricky's mom and dad
griped and grumbled
when the boys in the band
started playing.

Micky lived in a house with a lot of pets.

All the pets howled and yowled

when the boys in the band

started playing.

Nicky lived in an apartment.

Nicky's neighbors came to his door

and huffed and puffed

when the boys in the band

started playing.

"Can we practice in your grandma's basement anytime?" Ricky asked Kevin.

"You bet," said Kevin.

"Right," said Ricky. "You can be in the band then, Kevin. Okay, Micky?"

"Okay with me," said Micky.

"Okay, Nicky?"

"Okay with me," said Nicky.

"You're one of the band,
now, Kevin," said Ricky.
"G-r-e-a-t!" said Kevin,
and he smiled and smiled and smiled.

Chapter Two

Ricky and Micky and Nicky and Kevin

practiced every night

in Kevin's grandma's basement.

Kevin's grandma brought them drinks

and chocolate-chip cookies.

The band practiced
and practiced
and practiced.
Ricky and Micky and Nicky
got even better at singing.
Kevin still wasn't that great at singing.

Ricky and Micky and Nicky
got even better at dancing.
Kevin still wasn't that great at dancing.

Ricky and Micky and Nicky
all looked supercool.

Kevin didn't look cool at all.

But Ricky and Micky and Nicky

didn't want to push Kevin

out of the band.

They liked Kevin.

And they needed to practice

in Kevin's grandma's basement.

It was Kevin's grandma

who got the boys their first gig.

"My friend goes to this club.

They want a band for Saturday night.

I said I know a very good band.

Okay with you, boys?" said Kevin's grandma.

"Okay with me!" said Ricky.

"Okay with me!" said Micky.

"Okay with me!" said Nicky.

"G-r-e-a-t!" said Kevin.

"Thanks, Grandma!"

The band practiced even harder
for their Saturday night gig.

"What should we call our band?"

said Ricky.

"How about Ricky and Micky

and Nicky and Kevin?"

said Kevin.

"That doesn't sound very cool, Kevin,"

said Ricky.

"I'm not a very cool guy,"

said Kevin.

"Not like you, Ricky.

You're a real Mr. Cool.

And you, Micky.

You're a real Mr. Cool, too.

And you, Nicky.

Yet another

Mr. Cool."

"Mr. Cool," said Ricky.

He snapped his fingers.

"Excellent name!"

"Mr. Cool," said Micky.

He snapped his fingers.

"Terrific name!"

"Mr. Cool," said Nicky.

He snapped his fingers.

"Fantastic name!"

"Mr. Cool," said Kevin.

He tried to snap his fingers

but they got stuck.

It didn't matter.

"G–r–e–a–t,"

said Kevin,

and he smiled

and smiled

and smiled.

So the boys called the band Mr. Cool.

They didn't feel very cool

just before their first gig.

Ricky had problems with his voice.

Micky had problems with his feet.

Nicky had problems with his hair.

Kevin had lots and lots
and lots of problems.
"We're awful,"
said Ricky, Micky, and Nicky.
"We can't go on."
"I'm awful," said Kevin.
"But you guys are
excellent,
terrific,
fantastic.
We're going on.
And we're going
to be great."

So Mr. Cool played their first gig.

They were great.

Ricky and Micky and Nicky were excellent at singing.

Ricky and Micky and Nicky were terrific at dancing.

Ricky and Micky and Nicky looked fantastic.

Kevin still wasn't great at singing.

Or dancing.

Kevin still didn't look great either.

But he had a great smile.

And all the people in the club smiled, too.
They clapped and cheered
when the band took a bow.
Mr. Cool was a big success.

Chapter Three

Ricky and Micky and Nicky and Kevin

played at the club every Saturday night.

They were asked to play

at a lot of other clubs, too.

And school dances.

And cafés.

They even did a gig at a birthday party,

but that was just for Kevin's grandma.

Then one night a man named Mr. Rich came to hear the boys play.
Mr. Rich was well known in the music world.

The boys were very nervous

when they spotted Mr. Rich.

"Don't worry, guys," said Kevin.

"We'll be great."

Kevin smiled,

and Ricky and Micky and Nicky

smiled back.

They did their act in front of Mr. Rich.

Ricky and Micky and Nicky

were excellent at singing.

Ricky and Micky and Nicky

were terrific at dancing.

Ricky and Micky and Nicky

looked fantastic, too.

Kevin wasn't great at singing.

Kevin wasn't great at dancing.

Kevin didn't look great either,

despite his new hand-knit sweater.

"You boys are incredible," said Mr. Rich.

"You're a great band.

I want to sign you up.

Well . . . I want three of you."

He pointed at Ricky.

He pointed at Micky.

He pointed at Nicky.

He didn't point at Kevin.

He shook his head.

"Sorry, kid," said Mr. Rich to Kevin.

"I don't want you in the band."

Kevin stopped smiling.

He nodded sadly and walked away.

"Hang on, Kevin!" said Ricky.

"You're part of Mr. Cool.

I say you take all four of us, Mr. Rich

—or none of us.

Okay with you, boys?"

"Okay with me!" said Micky.

"Okay with me!" said Nicky.

Kevin didn't say anything.

But he smiled.

"Okay with me, too,"

said Mr. Rich, sighing.

Mr. Rich groomed the boys for stardom.

They made their first album.

Ricky and Micky and Nicky

were excellent at singing

on their first Mr. Cool album.

Kevin wasn't that great.

He sang very softly.

They made their first video.

Ricky and Micky and Nicky

were terrific at dancing

on their first Mr. Cool video.

Kevin wasn't that great.

He danced out of camera shot

most of the time.

They posed for their first
Mr. Cool photo shoot.
Ricky and Micky and Nicky
looked fantastic,
really supercool.
Kevin didn't look great.
He stood behind the other boys.

Mr. Rich set up a big concert tour
for Mr. Cool.

Ricky and Micky and Nicky
were *so* nervous.

Even Mr. Rich was a little bit nervous.

But Kevin told them not to worry.

"Stay cool, you guys," he said.

"They'll think we're great, you'll see."

MR. COOL TOUR
LONDON
NEW YORK
PARIS
LOS ANGELES
BARCELONA
PARAMUS

All the girls and boys did think
Mr. Cool was a great band.
They thought they were
excellent, terrific,
fantastic. Ricky and Micky
and Nicky and Kevin sang.
Ricky and Micky and Nicky
and Kevin danced.
Ricky and Micky
and Nicky and Kevin posed
in their new stage outfits.
Kevin chatted
to the audience.
"Hope you're having
a great time," he said,
and he smiled.

He saw his grandma at the back.

He waved.

Grandma waved back.

And all the girls and boys waved, too.

"We're having a great time, Kevin,"
they yelled.

"We love Mr. Cool.

We love Ricky.

We love Micky.

We love Nicky.

And most of all—we love you, Kevin!

We think you're g-r-e-a-t!"

Kevin smiled and smiled and smiled.

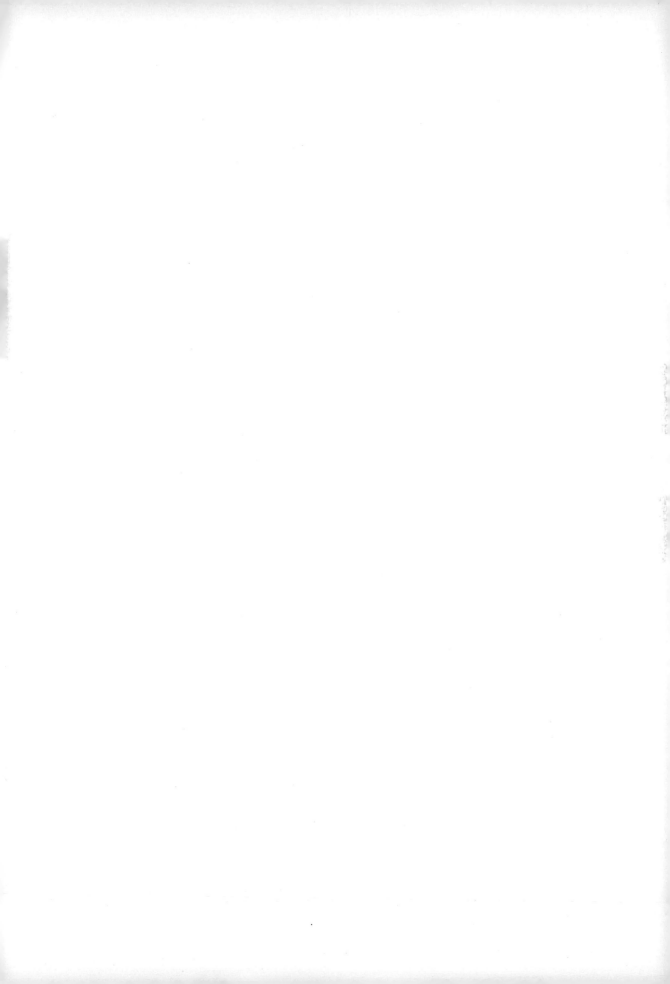

About the Authors and Illustrators

If you've enjoyed reading these stories, you may want to find out more about the people who wrote and illustrated them.

Jonathan Allen

Jonathan Allen played bass guitar in a band before he graduated from art school. Jonathan says, "When I was Joe Lion's age, I wanted to be a famous rock star, like the one in the poster on Brother Ben's bedroom wall." Now he is well known for illustrating children's books . . . but he still plays his bass guitar! Jonathan lives in Hertfordshire, England.

Andy Ellis

Andy Ellis has written and illustrated a lot of children's books. He also works on film animations for television, and his illustrations of Crocodile and Alligator are full of movement. He says, "Trying to make an alligator and a crocodile look friendly wasn't easy, but I hope the readers will think I've succeeded!" Andy lives in London, England.

Sally Grindley

Sally Grindley is an award-winning writer. Her own postman is not at all like the enthusiastic Giant Postman—he hates having to knock on the door to deliver a package. "He always comes early," says Sally, "and he knows I'm embarrassed by my just-got-out-of-bed, crumple-faced, tangle-haired state." Sally lives in Gloucestershire, England.

Stephen Lewis

Stephen Lewis graduated from art school in 1994 and has been illustrating children's books ever since. "I went to school with lads who formed a band," says Stephen. "They became just as successful as Mr. Cool—but none of them was quite like Kevin." Stephen lives in Cheshire, England.

Kara May

Kara May was born in Australia, and as a child she acted on the radio. She says, "Even though I am grown-up now, I am still the smallest in my family, so I know just how Joe Lion feels." Kara used to work in the theater and has written a lot of plays for children, but now she writes books full-time. Kara lives in London, England.

Nicola Moon

Nicola Moon was a science teacher before she began writing books. Nicola says, "When I was a child, I can remember helping to make cakes, just like Alligator." She says about JJ Rabbit, "I hope readers will make friends with JJ and his gang and enjoy sharing their adventures." Nicola lives in Wiltshire, England.

Ant Parker

Ant Parker is well known for his bright, colorful illustrations. He doesn't know any rabbits like JJ, but he does have a dog called Bramble who likes to look for adventure and then leaves big muddy pawprints all over the house. And Bramble looks just like JJ's friend Badger! Ant lives in London, England.

Wendy Smith

Wendy Smith has written and illustrated lots of books for children, and she also teaches art and illustration. Wendy is not afraid of her postman. She says, "I love to hear the letterbox rattle in the morning. I enjoy guessing who the letter is from, and wondering what news I'm going to read!" Wendy lives in London, England.

Jacqueline Wilson

Jacqueline Wilson is a favorite children's writer. Her books have won many awards, including the Smarties Book Prize. She says, "Kevin certainly doesn't look cool like the rest of the boys in the band—but he's so funny and friendly it doesn't matter a bit." Jacqueline has lived in Kingston-upon-Thames, England, since she was three.